A Sincere Love Failure Story

It's A true love story of Middle class boy

Vikram Pulipati

ISBN 978-93-5559-189-0
© Vikram Pulipati 2021
Published in India 2021 by Pencil

A brand of
One Point Six Technologies Pvt. Ltd.
123, Building J2, Shram Seva Premises,
Wadala Truck Terminal, Wadala (E)
Mumbai 400037, Maharashtra, INDIA
E connect@thepencilapp.com
W www.thepencilapp.com

DISCLAIMER: *The opinions expressed in this book are those of the authors and do not purport to reflect the views of the Publisher.*

Author biography

Myself VIkram stays in Hyderabad. To say about me its completely a true love story which has been failed at last.I can openly say this is true love story.The story which you read here in this book each and every line happened in life.Just enjoy this small love failure story which relates to you in any scene or any chapter.I hope you enjoys by reading this book. There is nothing more to say about me. A failure person saying about life and love in this book.Have a Happy reading :)

CONTENTS

CHAPTER 1 (BORN IN MIDDLE CLASS)

Let us start reading the book with a imagination.The great imagination skills gives us great feeling of story.

Think that this your story and imagine yourself in this character and read the book so that, this gives you a wonderful feeling.

This is real and true love story which is ended with failure,99.9% true love stories failes at the end.

Only 0.01% success because of sinceratiy in love of girl.

Let us begin the story.

in 06-01-1996 Andhra pradesh state there is village of Kalwakurthy,Mahabubnagar District.

I came on earth without knowing anything,obviously everyone will come on earth as the same.

But i doesnt know that on the other side of mine few kilometers far away on 10-10-1996 there is a princess coming on earth.

Days are passing my first birth day has been completed successfully, I still sees my first birthday album and laughes alot,

i think same thing you have done,changes alot from there to present.I was a fatty,chubby chubby born with

over weight but still my parents loved me alot. When i started walking.I still remember my dad usually says with me he loves sweets alot mainly

kalakhad which made with pure milk and sugar.i used to cross the main road lonely and travel to my dad shop,

he has sweet shop in that days and went to sweet shop and have the khalakhand in my childhood at the age of 3 .

slowly days are getting worse.Dad got lot of loss in the business graph went down.Financially our family didn't faced any good days.

Dad decided to travel to Hyderabad for better future.Sold all the assests.

CHAPTER 2 (MAHANAGARAM HYDERABAD)

Days are not upto mark in out family.Still I didn't ask my dad how you started the days in hyderabad.

Because I didn't want to remind any trouble days to my father.

My Schooling started in Hyderabad (Ram Nagar).Dad doesn't with the life he is living ,the only thing I

remember upto now. I slowly started growing up doesn't know any struggles which my father had.

We have changed many places in hyderabad according to my father work place.My father makes the excellent sweets and namkin.

He is the Master in Sweet Shops.Everywhere he worked he earned a very good name.

One fine day I still remeber I think its in my 4th class standad. when I was playing in school I was broken my Hand.

When I am trying to move fingers it was not,I don't know anything.I doesn't feel any pain of it.

Silently I came to home sat silently.Came to mom and said,trying to movie this hand but its not moving mom,

Mom slapped me and asked what happened what you did.

playing in the school ground and it has been broken i think,but you dont worry it will set

Mom cried alot we both went to father work place in sweet shop near to our house.

I still see the dads inside cry and remember it.Dad took me to kapol cuts,one of the famous for broken hands,legs.

We travelled in bus to there,my father holded my hand.we went there dad took token requested him that he is small boy please can you send us first.

I still feels that dad pain,how he cried inside, how much tense is at that movement.

Next my turn there.I said to him nothing happened uncle just felt down.

He took oil and started massaging over my left hand.Then it started paining really in my life,first time I have seen what is the pain.

Everyone beside me went off with my sound. He cracked my bones and set the bone in correct place.

It took almost an hour for it.He said bring regularly every week till 4 weeks.bone has been broken and it takes time nearly one month.

Then I thought again I should come here,instead of broking the bone ,he is broking my hand with pain alot.

Later Days are passing.But every day mom tries to cook calcium and protien food for me.Chicken,eggs like other things,I still didn't remember but mom

taken care of everything. Even when dad comes brings some fruits.Didn't went to school.Every day there is a wonder day for me like

eating and sleeping.In this holidays I maded my own purse with paper.I started my first saving of 1 rupee in it.

The time has again came to go change the bandage. I wented to dad shop dad given me rings(chakodi) to eat. I still remember to this day.

We boarded the bus and conductor asked for one rupee change. Dad asked me give me one rupee change which I have given you morning.The main

Wrong thing I have done is showing my purse to dad. I opened my purse and given one rupee with anger and thrown purse over there.

Every seen us and shock when I was scolding dad. The best movement I haven't forget upto now.

Slowly Days have been passing with some smiles,fights and same tough financial days.

CHAPTER 3 (LOST MY BROTHER)

Upto now I were topper in the school.I have everything in minded like each and everypoint I can read,write and fast learning.

I didn't introduce my family right,we are four member's my dad,mom me and my small brother.Usually everyone knows brothers

fighting would be more dangerous. It is like third world war in small family. I am dad favourite son and my brother is Mom favourite son. He is one year difference to me.

I still didn't remember any incidents and sweet memories with him. Why I don't understand.In my childhood but my brother is my super hero.

When mom says buy something, I goes to buy it and along with it I would buy choclate or biscuit.But what my brother does you know,

when mom says buy something to my brother he goes buy only the thing which my mom said, gives balance change to my mom.

Here its the difference between him and me.

But in my life I still now didn't except this would be happen or happened.Don't know why god takes back the only one which we have.

Suddenly don't know what happened to my brother,he felt down.Everyone mom dad are in tense running to one hospital and from there taking to another hospital.

Dad still in tension don't understand what to do.Doctors confirms that my brother got pneumonia.

I were at my aunty home.two to three days have been passed.My uncle came and said your brother has been dead.

I only remember this word.That's it everything colapsed. I don't know what happening. Everything happening in front of me but I still doesn't remeber

anything in my life. Brought brother to home. He is lying down but not opening eyes.Mom trying to wake up but he is not getting up.

Dad sat lonely a side.Tears in everyone face.I were in tense and I am not understand my brother is sleeping like that.I tried to wake up him but doesn't response.

Even though I asked my mother. I will buy him his favourtie biscuits ,tell him to wake up but he didn't .

My brother cheated me and left me alone in this world saying to fight alone with the problems.Still now I don't where he is.

His last funeral happened,Dad lifted with his hands went off,I didn't know at that time where is going.At that time I am still in thought that my brother comes back in sometimes.

But upto now I didn't seen him,later I understood that he is no more..........!

CHAPTER 4 (WORST DAYS IN MY LIFE)

I don't why god plays a carrom board with our lifes.After I lost my brother I have seen so many changes in our family.We are three member's now.

We have changed the house relocated to other place. Dad addicted to alchol. Already we are effected so much with financial situtation in that dad addicted to

alchol is getting more difficulties to us.I entered in 6th class and slowly now everything is understanding what is family and what is days which we are facing.

My studies completely lost. I don't what I am studying and what I am writing. After losing my brother all my days are black days for me. Mom started going in to work

to get some money to home. Dad money has not enough to run the family, school fees.When I first time seeing mom working. I felt so much bad. I presonally cried alot.

Mom wake ups at morning 5 AM cooks the food makes me get ready for school,with me she comes to schools drops me over there and she went's off to work.

Days are very worst in life, in past when I comes home mom will be at home,throughs the bag away and mom gives me food get ready. But when I goes home dad won't be at

home and mom also,this remembers me brother a lot. Slowly I also addicted to alone life.

The Summer holidays have came. Mom used to work a 1 rupee coin box industry. I decided go to work with my mom. I have dream of buying carrom board for me and music player (Tape recorder box) for my dad. At that days we don't have TV in home. I still remember on my friend commented on me. We stays in one small room. my friend said with me your house is smaller than my bath room. At that I felt very badly.

When knowing family position, how can I ask in home to buy this things, so I decided to go work with my mom and earn some money

and buy this things. In summer holidays every goes to ground to play cricket but I used to go with my mom to work.

Days are passing and I earned 500 Rupees per month in those days. In that company my work also almost my did.

I burnt my houses.Because I forgotted to wear gloveses.After getting enough money I quit the job and went to shopping with my dad.

I brought the carrom board with my own salary in my 7th class.I brought the tape recorder with my own salary too. but I forgot there need to be casets to play it. But luckly dad brought casets. Later I understood that to play carrom board there is another player needed.

Carrom board went up on shelfs. we back to school.slowly days are passing. I entered in to the 10th standard.

CHAPTER 5 (10TH STANDARD STORY)

Everyone's rememberable days are 10th days. The same I have in my life.My close frineds in my life till I remember in my life is two memebers Vineel and Prabhu.

This both are my souls in my 10th standard. We enjoyed alot in our school days. life is like anything in those days. We are the kings of the school.Vineel is the topper of the school and I am also Topper of the class from last. My studies is like abced in 10th standard. My Tension started in life about 10th standard board exams. But Vineel helped me in my school

days to get of the exams in every time.I failed in school level cricket competition but VIneel supported me. When every time others blames that you are failure product , vineel comes

forward and gives me enough support.Each and every time I used to Tease prabhu but he supports me. I am a poetry writer in school days. When anyone tries to impress a girl in class they makes me to write a poetry on behalf of them. Ashwanth is one of my friend who always pulls me up by indirectly providing me opportunites. my 10th batch is evergreen.

slowly 10 th is coming to end I realised how relationships are important in life, When my friend vineel said that from tomorrow onwards we can't I cried alot, we hug each other and

I only know how much I cried. After completing my 10th results are out. almost I crossed with boarder with just 66% . At that time

when I sees my dad face, clean bowled I am. From my school days only I have dream to became Film Director. I slowly understand that if we can make shortfilms

we can get good future. But Buying a camera in those days is not an easy. It almost costs of 55,000 rupees. With this marks I can't go and ask dad

to buy me a camera. He will surely slap me.At that time dad kept his own sweet shop with small budget. Slowly I thought we are again getting to older good days.

So every day I dream about buying camera and making shortfilms.But, don't know how to make it possible.Started my Intermedicate with MEC group in

Omega Junior College (Habsiguda,Hyderabad.) Already I am in week of maths means my dad put me in MEC. Doesn't understand how to make it possible,

New friends,new life. The Most dangeours and important step in life is Intermediate. But I was failed in using it.

I was completed intermediate first with playing,enjoying days but unfortunetly one backlog which is mathematics.

Then again when I see my dad face. I understood that I am at the edge of stadium.

CHAPTER 6 (LOVE BEGINS)

Those are the Intermediate first year holidays. Beside my dad shop there is the type institute. In afternoon times

I used to go to that shop and learn typing.Slowly when days are passing I was perfect in typing in all segments.

One fine dad. The typing Madam said I am going out for work and I will come in the evening please look at the students.

When the sister having works she will hand over me and she will go for work. As its holidays anyhow I am free. I will enjoy typing.

Its almsot an evening suddenly one girl comes in and asks is madam not there. I replies madam is not there went out tell me

"How can I help"

I am new joining today is my first class.

I replies ok no problem come in and take your seat.

I started saying her the first class instructions and how to do typing.

In my life this is the first time talking with a girl who don't know to me.My mind doesn't calls her as sister.

First time when I have seen her, she is in white dress. One of my favourite colour is white.

Slowly I am trying to see her. I took beside her chair and I started typing, doing practice.

She asks a doubt. I helped her and I enjoyed some feeling when I am talking with her.

The class time has been over she went off.

Next day............

I am waiting for her to come.She comes in and I pray for the god to make her sit beside me.

Madam asks yesterday who teached you class and she searches for me in the class.

She replies he teaches me class.

Madam replies :

Ok no problem,

Madam Tells me,

Sit beside him, He will tell you next class today.He already completed all classes and expert in typing.

Then I thanked god for this.

She Came and sat beside me, she asked my name and i replied vicky and I asked her name and she replied her name

(sorry for not disclosing her original name because I don't her to face any problems because of this book)

Let us assume her name is Rani

My imagination started. But I am only in confuse that is it love or infactutation ?

But slowly I started talking with her. I enjoyed alot her company.

Days are passing, its almost one months has been our and its coming to end of the course time.

CHAPTER 7 (PROPOSAL DAY)

My heart beat is raised alot. I don't know what happen to me. Her classes are coming to end.

I don't know what to do. I felt almost this are last days for me. I slowly took my smart phone which is china made.

At those days 2G network is more than enough. I have downloaded a image, which having the quote of

'I CAN'T LIVE WIHTOU YOU"

Slowly in talking with her I have shown the image to her.Said How is this. She sees and says nice

whats the special in this.

Then I understood that its more tougher that I think.Then I said to read the quote in it. Then after few minutes she understood

that I am proposing her. She says that I can't believe love all this. How can I love you ,just you are my friend.

Later I ask her we have more two days classes think and tell me I said.

I have given promise to her that I am not loving you for the time pass. I can treat you as my mother.

I have decided and I am giving you the promise.

Tomorrow I will wait for your response here only in class.

And this is my phone number. I will wait for your text.

Later I have went off from there. Day has been changed and she didn't came to the class from next day.

My heart is broken don't know what is understand.

I thought is there anything wrong in me.

I have checking my mobile each and every minute for her mobile.

SLowly I opened the registration book in typing school and I have checked for her number.

Her mother number is feeded in the book.

I just taken that number and saved in my contact list but I have not dare to call that number.

5 days have been passed and I have not seen her........

CHAPTER 8 (ANGEL IS BACK)

Its been almost a week passed. One day typing sister said I was going on work stay today in the institute.

I was completely mood and not understanding what to do. I was unable to give classes to other's and clarify doubts.

Slowly one girl enter in to the institute and that is she.But she came with her mother. I don't understand what to do.

Her mother waits outside and she cames in and asks is the madam not there?

I replies : No Madam, went out.

She comes closer to me and says Suddenly next day morning we went off to shirdi.

I didn't have phone to say you the news.

I really felt so bad. I also missed you so much. Each and every minute I dreamed about you in trip.

Yesterday only we came back from shirdi, Yes I accept you.

I miss you and sorry, night I will do normal message from mom phone.

Bye take care........

This are the words which I still remember.I will remeber this words till my last breath.

I have checked clock each and every minute when the sunset will happen and when she will text me.

The days almost comes to end but I didn't got any text from her end.

This made me cry alot.

Its has been past almost three days but I didn't got any text from her end.

My mood is completely off and days end with tears in eyes.............

CHAPTER 9 (SHE TEXTED ME)

Later after couple of days. I suddenly got text from her number stating Hi.

I immediately replied to her why there is no text from your end from last couple of days.

She replied me stating that I was tense and still in thinking that is this love true ?

This is the first text message between her and me.

Later we both came to one understand that we shouldn't break our love in any time in the love.

My intermediate sencond year started again.

She is Intermediate first year.

Those days I still remember till now.

When first time she went to the college,to meet her I went in the rain in the evening,

There is the heavy rain. In the evening 4 o clock I went in the bus to her college and standard outside of

there college little bit far away just to see her.

Till now I remember her first smile at me.

I think everyone who loves her girl friend remembers her first smile at us.

Every day I used to go her by bunking my college to see her.

Her college is 2 kilometers away from my college.

There are days daily 100 text limits has been ended in just one hour.

We used to count more how many text messages are left.

we used to save one text message for night to text message as good night,because without this message

I and she won't sleep...

CHAPTER 10 (FIRST BIRTHDAY OF MY RANI)

Its a countdown for me.My girl friend first birthday is going to come in couple of days.

I don't know what to give her a gift. This should be her lift time memory.We upto now didn't went out.

First time in my life I asked her to come with me outing on her birthday.First she rejects,says I can't bunk

the class and come with you because in college register my parents number is there.

I have given advice to her,in college register your mother number is there right, so just bring her phone.

If phone gets we can lift and talk the call.Slwoly after lot of conversation she came with me for outing.

But I too have the same position, I have lot of tension where to take her, what gift I should give to her.

Alot of questions running in my mind, I keep on asking advices for my frineds who already having the girl friend and took

her outing on there birthdays.

At those days. 3G is running and I grabbed my friend phone for outing. Because to have first selfie with her.

Some how I managed the amount for outing around 1000rs.

My life time feeling its. Because going with a girl outing is first time in my life.

We boarded the bus first and went to chilkur balaji temple. Because I have planned her birthday with time to time.

Later after taking the blessings of the god.We went from there to Golconda fort.

Thats me second time visiting golconda after my school picnic.

When I came first time to golconda its not beautiful but second time when I went with my Rani its fantastic.

I felt that again I can rule the Hyderabad with my Rani from there.

Later once we come out there are so many bangles shop and rings shop outside the golconda.

Its not original but for pure hearts its original.....

CHAPTER 11 (MY FIRST GIFT TO HER)

We both went to one shop over there near golconda fort and we had some shopping like purchase of

bangles and some other small items. We sat on one bench over there. Still I didn't had any gift for her.

Later I went small shop infront of us and I purchased small gift which is Ring for her

The ring is filled with white stone and I feel like this ring is equal to diamond ring.

Slowly I came near to her and I had the word with her.

Sorry, I didn't have any beautiful or precious gift to you,

I tried so much but money didn't got adjusted.

But now which I am giving you is from bottom of my heart.

I can't live without you in my life,at the same time I can't imagine in the place of you other girl and in the place of me another boy for you.

Will you be with me forever ?

I showed the ring to her.

She cried,tears are out from her eyes and me too.

She holds my hand asks me...

You only please wear this ring to me.

She holds my hand tightly and says

"I LOVE YOU FOREVER"

I never forget this word from her.

She says I never remove this ring from my hand.

CHAPTER 12 (DREAMING ABOUT MARRIAGE LIFE)

There are so many happy days comes in my life after she enters in my life.My family position also slowly

getting stabilized.Daily morning I used to travel with her till college and I comes back to my college.

Those days are my life golden days.We started imaging as other do about marriage life.

We decided to have a best life in upcoming days with our own house, two kids and out both families.

She is also alone daughter to her family. We are three and her family also three members.

So we have decided to have 3 floors house. Ground floor is for my dad and mom. First floor is for there mom and dad,

finally top floor is for us. Those imaginations are really gives boost for our life.

Slowly days are passing and we both are having happy life

but we didn't expected that there are summer holidays infront and two months we can't meet.

Those made me cry alot for us.Because without seeing for one day only we can't

That too without meeting for two months is can't possible even in dreams.

SUMMER HOLIDAYS HAVE BEEN STARTED

She doesn't have her mother phone with her in summer holidays because,her mother wents to job,

she used to go to his uncle home and there he sister will be there (bhabhai daughter)

Daily morning I walk infront of there house to see her.

Weekly every thursday morning and evening we went to sai baba temple near to her house to see her.

Slowly I concentrated on my dream camera also. I thought I should not miss this summer holidays chance and

I started working in the Internet center beside my house.......!

CHAPTER 13 (STEPS TO MY DREAM)

I started working in the Internet cafe beside my house for full time morning 9-10 shift. The brother is so nice and agreed to pay me 9000 per month.

This boosted me and I said to my dad that I will work there for full time for 2 months in summer and I will buy camera in EMI.

The internet cafe is so good that without keeping any money I was able to access around the world through net and I learned so many things

like c,c+ java and other things like online job applications.Here my typing is improved alot because daily

we will have DTP works over there.

Slowly days are passing, I said to brother give me two months salary at a time because my dream is to buy camera.

The brother already know about my film direction dream and he accepted and he doesn't broke the promise.

But anyhow my intermediate results have came and I have passed my backlog and intermediate second year also with same

second class.

I didn't bothered about my results.Before checking my results I have checked my Rani resutls and She is passed

first year with first class.That Made me so much.

She called me from her mother phone and I still remember her words

Bangaram Nuvvu nennu idharam pass

(Darling you and me both pass)

Slowly My summer holidays has been over. I got my salary and we went to reliance store near my house to buy a camera

Then I understood that to buy a camera we need credit card in EMI or there should be cibil score.

Then All my hopes came down.

In my circle I contacted all the member's to help but no one came forward.

My Tenth friend vineel also helped me 1000 rupees for camera.

but the amount which i have will work for only downpayment....

CHAPTER 14 (MY BIRTHDAY)

But I never quit this,I have went to one brother who is near to my house.I knows about me and my struggles,

He came with me immeditely once I ask and we both went to again reliance store and brother with his Credit card brought camera for me

Canon 700D with two lens whole kit.The next point is emi,monthly 3750.

One question raised in my mind how to pay emi for 12 months that too 3750 per month.

My only one thing is for anything we should not depend on parents, If I want I should buy it orelse not.

I entered in to Degree. My Rani is in Intermediate second year.

Everything is fine upto now,Again I went to internet cafe and I said to the brother from evening 5 to night closing I will work brother

give me monthly 4000 . Brother without second thought said Ok.

This Made me happy but I am missing little bit time with my Rani.

In My degree first Year dad broght the bike, I still remember its Glamour bike.

But I wish to travel in bus because I can spend some time with her.

Still now I don't understand why god has given 24 hours a day for all.

Because the days are keep on passing like a minutes.

With my camera I started my first shortfilm.

Slowly everything is going on happily.

We are upgraded from text messages to whatsapp.

This makes me happy because unlimited messages but limited internet at that time.

Jio network hasn't entered in the market.

The days.Which is my birthday.I still remeber, we both have made the decision at any cost on our both birthdays

we should go outing. Thats our second outing.We went to Movie Andhala Rakshashi Movie.

In the Intervel I went to bring snacks. But I am still affraid to leave her alone.

Once I came back with snacks I have seen some different smile on her face. I still remeber that smile on her face.

I asked her why are you charming like a diamond.She holds my hand tightly.Kisses my hand and says happy birthday dear.

She gives a gift box. I really shocked.That's first birthday gift. Because no one given me gift upto now.

I opened that box and there is coffee cup inside printed with my photo and my camera in my hand. That was first photo from our shortfilm.

I really shocked and there is smiling ball also in it.

This is the first gift from her to me and this time went on bike because its my brithday and I took her first time on bike to outing...

CHAPTER 15 (FIRST BREAK UP IN OUR LOVE)

In every true love this day will surely comes.We didn't even expected this in our life.

Those are horror days in my life.I can't Even re-imagine those days.Slowly days are passing we are so much happy in life.

Again there is a holidays came in our life.I have completed my first year of degree and she has completed intermediate.

We have decided to be in phone touch everyday and our regular spots like meeting in temple.But I have tension that she won't be available of phone everytime

so I brought a new phone for her from my savings second hand and I have given her.

The days are going smoother but one fine day her bhabhai son, his brother revealed our matter in there family.

That's it blasted our love.Her uncle and parents beaten her so much to tell about me who is he.

But she hided about me deleted phone texts and hidden the phone which I have given.

She cried alot.But her mother beaten her alot even his drunken father too.

I still don't understand how she hideen the pain in her.

There Bhabhai (uncle) beaten her ruthlessly to know about me but she even didn't told name.

Later they grabbed the ring from her hand thrown away.

For this she broken her heart didn't had any food and hospitilised.

Her mother took a promise from her that she won't meet me again in life and won't talk with me.

Later slowly she recovered from those pains.But those days are horrible to me because I didn't any text from her.

I didn't seen her for three months.

Later she joined in Women's degre college which is near to my college.

But even though when I tried to meet her she avoids me says that its all over don't ever try to meet me,

she given the phone back to me which I have given to her.

CHAPTER 16 (WAITING FOR GOOD DAYS)

Literaly I am not able to survive those days.Daily I tried to talking her but she says on my face that don't show me your face to me in my life.

Those words are broken me alot.I really appreciate her because when our love matter came to know in her house she didn't told about me

even my name or address when they beat her with belt.

I waited for her almost 3 months to talk with her.Suddenly I was meet with accident and I felt down from bike.

Few days I didn't wen to college and I was in home. I was completely unhappy. My hand was broken again. This is the second time for the same left hand.

I even didn't step out of my house.Later after few days with the bandage to my hand only I went to the college.

I was on my friend bike,Unable to take the bus because of the hand pain.We have a spot where in my rani college street only we use to have tea and tiffins.

She is crossing the tea stall and slowly she looked for me and she stopped while walking by seeing bandage to my hand.

immediately tears are out of her eyes. her friends grabbed her to the college.Immediately I got a call from her friend phone.

I was tense to lift the call and I didn't lifted the call.Again I got a call from same number. I didn't lifted the because I were in tense that she said I shouldn't talk with her.

She I am crossing her college,because to go to my college I need to cross her college.

From Above her college window her friend called me loudly and said.

Brother, Rani is crying alot,lift the call immediately.

Then Immediately I lifts the call and thats her voice, after so many months I heard her voice.

She didn't given me one second to talk.Just she keep on scolding me what happened to your hand,are you mad,stupid there are so many words.

I doesn't feel its a bad words or scolding. But when I hear her voice thats time I was reborn.

CHAPTER 17 (LET'S RESTART)

After Completing the horrible days. I need to restart and gear up the life for second innings in our love,

Next day only I took her to outing.I cried alot because almost I thought its all over.After so many days listening

her voice given me rebirth.

We have enjoyed alot in the love. There are so many clashes between us at the same time mutual understanding between us.

Days are passing slowly and there is the dusserra holidays.First time after meeting her.On her birthday we didn't went out because its an dusserra holidays.

But I feel thats an good for us,because I have seen her in saree for the first time in my life.

She came to the temple in saree.

Thats the wonderful and important day in my life.Still now I can't forget that imagination.

She is in blue saree with white flowers design on it.She is having curley hair.Cool weather.No make up natural face.Just her smile is enough for her to tell about beauty in her face.

The smile which she given me is equal to 10000 dollars worth money.I can doesnt forget. On her birthday she made me archana on my name in temple.

Because she usually says to me you should celebrate my brithday and my birthday is your's birthday.

First I decided in my life, after our marriage she always should wear a saree. Because short girls looks awesome in saree.

This is not an sexual opinion,its an pure love.But later once she comes to college I have given her a gift.

Which is of chain contains letter V.She wear that and in home they asks she says its her mom name .Because her mom name starts with V

But she always asks me to give the gift of ring,even it is small 5 rs or 10 rs, but I didn't dare to give her because,if again I gives

anything same happens like past means, I can't dare.

We had so many days passes in our life.

There are so many festivals comes in life like dusserra,bonalu bathukamma.

Everytime I waited for the festival because to see her in saree.I think she is the worlds most beautiful Angel in Saree.

CHAPTER 18 (VR4U ANTI RAGGING ORGANISATION)

Everything in life comes to an end at certain point.Its time to complete.Its my Graduation final Year.

In the College days only I started VR4U ANTI RAGGING ORGANISATION to help women.

We started this organisation with help of my degree friends. With the help of this organisation we have travelled to

three to four colleges in the first month only with the help of padmavathi madam (child welfare) and local police station SI sir's to

conduct seminars on ragging in colleges and awareness. Those days are wonderfull as I took it as challenge

and became social activist. With our pocket moneys we travelled organised events in colleges.

Some colleges supported us and some are not.

VR means V for Vicky and R for Rani

By combining our names I have formed VR4U organisation.

Slowly me and my team nishanth,naveen,shashi,mahesh and few others joined in the hand to help blood donation camp at our degree college.

That was an awesome experience for us.

Because in the degree age only we took social responsibilites and everyone helped us in making this success.

We tied up with Thalaseemia Organisation to make this successfully.

Slowly everything sets down and I this process I were not given proper time for Rani.

But she doesn't miss understand me and helped me alot in making this success by giving her pocket money, scholarship to me.

Every rupee of her savings given to me to make success of my ideas.

We nishanth and naveen we though we are poor middle class family

We tried to make this happen.

Chapter 19 (I felt Shy)

I felt shy.In my life I don't want to face this situation again.When we are successfully in life with our org. We got very good name with this organisation near premises.

My frineds are very super active and next decided to conduct next seminar in women's degree college which is my rani studying college.

I really shocked with my friends decision. But I came to know that there any many other colleges boys teasing there because its an women college.

So I didn't step back and we went to start the seminar in that college.But, before seminar day we use to go to each and every classes and we will inform about the next seminar

important things and benefits. ALways I use to go to each and every college and on the dias I use to speak. Because I am stage speaker and I am having good knowledge about it.

When we are going to each and every class in that college , I requested to my friend nishanth to take next class speech by him. But all my friends refused because they all know that My rani is in that class.I slowly entered in there class and requested lecture that we are from anti ragging org. need two minutes of your class time to address the class. The lady lecture permitted us and I have move forwarded to inform them about the tomorrow seminar.I really felt shy and I am unable to speak anything properly because

rani sat in the middle of the class. All the class girls are smiling inside because they all know that I am rani lover, rani without blinking her eyes she is looking me.

I am not understanding what to do over there. My speech complete collapsed but however, I have managed and escaped from that class.

Later after completing there class rani meet me outside in bus stop and asks me why are feeling shy? why can't you talk properly.

I smiled and replied you be in my position and I will be in your position and then you will know what happened at that movement. She smiles and says I can't speak infront of all.

Those words and smiles from her are memorable for me.We have successfully completed in seminar in there college and in that college I have not given any speech.

I have brought my college female girls to host the event. Luckily it went well.

Chapter 20 (IT'S MY JOB TIME)

Its almost my graduation ending time. Upto there I didn't faced anything difficult except one time break up in our love.Everyone should be face this in life.

we have records which need to write. There are so many records I don't know how to complete it. Rani took all my records she completed my records.

She supported me in everything. She pushed me to go to college in last days to get of it.Everything going well but I am Missing her alot.We have decreased using our

phones. Hours of talking time in phone came to minutes. Just HI and bye messages. Slowly days have been passed and Its time for campus placements.

I am in mega drive of campus placements which has been organised by our college. We got selected in nearly 3 colleges because of my typing skills and communications skills.

My lectures pushed me forward and I got easily selected. But I didn't expect this. I started getting continous calls from Rani when I was interview, I am unable to lift the call.

Nearly there are 50+ Missed calls in just 1 hr. When I came out and tried to return call back here mobile switch off.

I am in tense I don't know what to do. Upto now I didn't hear her mobile as switch off. Later after few hours I got return call back from her.

With the tension in my face I lifted her and She continously keep on crying. I am not understanding what to do and how to stop her.later after few minutes and convincing her she clam down. She explained me about her family situtation.

There is a matches seeing her in home and told her to stop studies immediately.She had the fight in the home. She with her uncle,mom and dad openly that after completing her MBA only she will do marriage.Her mother came to slap her, and asks that are you still loving him?

She cries alot , her father came forward and said ok you study untill you study after that only we will do marriage.

Later next day we meet and had the discussion about our life. She said with me that our castes are different, I can't leave parents and come with you.My mother is expecting good job,own house and well settled family.She says that try to settle in life as soon as possible we have two years in hand.

She went off from there silently. first time in my life she left me alone in one place and went.That made me cry alot. Immediately in the evening I texted her that tomorrow onwards

I am going to job and as soon as possible I will settle to marry you. The next minute I got her selfie saying I love you bava .... That boost is enough and I have joined job in Hinduja global solutions as customer representative.

CHAPTER 21 (IT'S TIME TO SET)

My job career is running very well with good employee name in office. I have succeed in office in all parameters.As this is mainly linked with communication and

typing. As I worked for customer chat support.But I were unhappy with the salary which I gets. Its an almost 15k and In home I would give 10k. with just 5k savings

I can't get settle as soon as possible. There Rani is getting tense alot regarding my job and our life.Already its been almost 1 year has been completed but I didn't have enough money in my hand. Then I decided to enter in the business. I have had the word with my dad and he said ok for the businesss. My dad given me some amount,some how with credit card amount and my savings all placed in one place and I opened on my father name business.Which is srinivasa communications. Which deals with mobiles,money transfer,xerox , internet and all online applications.This helped me alot but rani was not happy because her mother doesn't like business and it is not stable.But I were tried to make understood rani and she accepted my business after few months.By god grace I got very good amount of profits in the business and all my family got settled financially in just 6 months.My 6 months salary I would get in only one month in business. Because I got benefit here is I am having experience in this business as I worked as employee in this business.Slowly Rani was happy and I was happy. We got one hope that we would get settle in next one year.I slowly started buying the things in my family. I just kept in mind which I am buying should get use for Rani.

I brought 55 Inch TV , so That Rani can get entertainment in big screen

I brought washing machine of 35k, so that once rani comes to my house she won't need to wash clothes.

I brought sofa, so that rani happily sit and relax.

I brought cooler so that rani won't get sweat.

I brought bed, so that rani won't need to sleep down.

Each and everything I keept only in mind of rani.

My another dream is to buy a car for dad.But I don't want to go for EMI. So I planned to buy a second hand car for my in red colour,because rani favourite.

On my parents marriage day I brought second hand car as there anniversary gift.

This made me so much happy,because now my dad dream came to true. My dad travelled on cycle to his work place,

Now he has his own business,owner of store,own Scooty and now car.

This Made me so so so much happy. but not with me for long time.........

CHAPTER 22 (IT'S AN FAILURE)

For a middle class boy and sincere people,harding working people happiness won't stay for long time.This happens in everyone.Everything is in my control I feels.I didn't seen loss in my business even in single day. Astrology said business won't be that much benefit for you but I didn't bothered about it and I entered into the business to make it happened.Every one my friend said you made the right decision in your life to get the success in desired time. I felt so much happy and I felt that I will also get marry with rani because now I have everything which there family want.Its been almost two years over. I doesn't wish to buy the builder constructed property because I and Rani has one dream. We need to build our own house. So with my savings I took all my savings out,My chittis all funds and all my dad money and we brought open land of 100 sq.yards. So in next year with loan or buy saving we can start construction over there. Rani felt very much happy and she says when marriage topic gets on in family I will talk about you. From my end everything is clear because I can easily make ok with my family.Its been 7+ years of love has been passed in our life. But I don't know it would be last year for our love.

Slowly Days are passing and I got a call from rani one fine day and said someone is coming to home to see me today.

She said with me that once they come and go I will tell with dad about our love.I said before coming only say why after coming. She says if before comes all get messy, let them come and I will say once they went off.

I said ok you plan according to your family situtation but don't make this fail.She said me a word , only you should touch my body, no one have the rights for it.

I felt confidence that she can make and I am preparing for counter action if they comes to my business place.Rani said that Untill I call you, you don't call me .

I have waited for two days and I thought there mind be some issues happening.Let her wait for her call.

I have waited for his call almost but I didn't got any call and 5 days has been passed. I tried to recall and its switch off.

I am completely shocked. I tried to go in there street and I asked her friend about her. They said me that they are in there house its locked.

I am not understanding what to do and I am completely in blank. After a week I got a call from her. I picked her call and I got a ans from her. I have tried but my parents are not accepting our. you please delete my number,our photos,memories,lettters everything and don't try to black mail me. By listening her words I have shocked and I am not understanding what to do.She disconnected the call and when I retry its switch off.....................

CHAPTER 23 (ITS AN END OF LOVE STORY)

I have tried so many ways to talk with her but I didn't find any route. My mind is out of control. I tried contacting with her frineds but they said we are also unable to get in touch with her brother.My Patience dead, I directly called her mother and asked that I am loving Rani, why are you trying to break our love. She disconnected the call. The next day her Uncle (Bhabhai) came to my store and asked me do you recognize me. I said I am sorry sir, I don't. He said I am Rani uncle.You called Rani mother. May I know the reason ?.I replied you all know everything but you all trying to break our love.I just want to talk with her. He replies to me stating that, I already the word with Rani and she said that she doesn't loves ,she just did casually upto now but she doesn't mean for marriage. I replied, how can you say that uncle,let me hear that words from her.The he says ok I will go home and call you. She will only say you.

I immediately replied, I want to meet her and talk with her 2 minutes. If she says that she is not loving me I won't coming in her live again.

The time has arrived one evening, we meet at one place,she comes with her mother,father and uncle.I went with one of my well known brother.

She came a side little bit fare away and I asked her,look in to my face.

She starring at me.

I asked her, are you not loving me.

She said, No I am not loving me.

I asked her, then what we did from 7+ years?

She said, I just did time pass with you, I never mean to marry you.Already I liked the person which my parents brought to me.Why would I will marry. You are a fool.

This words from her broken my heart there.

My well known brother asked one question to her. See sister, only one question to you, no lover says this wrong. you don't need to worry anyone, you don't need to worry about your parents, they may beat you,they warn you that they will do suicide,but here I am there and I am responsible of there life and your's. Give a promise on vicky death,you didn't love him?

she promises on my death and say yes I didn't love him,just did timepass. I only loves the person who came in my life now, which my parents shown.

Brother asked. If vicky died now you won't bother?

she replies, why would I bother if he died now?

That's it my life is ended there.............................

CHAPTER 24 (FALL OF DREAMS)

The next minute of that, my heart stopped beating for few seconds. I really praies the god that if that would be a bad dream.But it's not.Slowly I am getting down in my life.

She got engaged in life. I lost my business and I have see losses in my business.I sold my car. I sold my property.My family came under debts.Everything which I try seriously also get failed. All my lucky charm is she and after she going away from my life I am a failure product.I Sold 50% of my business. I sold everything which I am having.

I literally begged there friends for photo, there friends sent me her engagement photo and she is so much happy in it.My father doesn't understand why I am behaving like that.She changed her number. Wedding cards have been printed,marriage has been over, within 8 months only she got a boy in hand.One thing I won't understand about this girls.Suppose let us assume she got married on force of there parents but she can't get the pregnant on force of there parents right?

My question any boy married any girl,he won't touch her body until she heartfully permits.

When in love before marriage she said with a word. No one can touch this body except you. You have all rights of this ?

How that rights has been shifted easily.No husband touches his wife when she heartfully says ok.

Lets us leave about this.

Because this makes me alot of pain. After that upto now I have not seen her. Its been almost 4 years has been passed. I am waiting for single text from her end that,I truly loved you but my family made me like this,but I still didn't get this.

Still now I have her new number. But I won't did any call because I feels that my love is not true or I failed in showing proper love to her.

Don't know but I still loves her till my last breath.

I still didn't got married. I am in memories of her.I can't blame or scold anything her.Because I can't see her crying.

Where ever she stays,she should be happy. Its my pray to god.

Always love you and miss you dear.

regards

vikram

VR FOR ....